W9-BMU-072

MARCUS PFISTER was born in 1960 in Bern, Switzerland. After attending art school in Bern and subsequently training as a graphic designer, he worked from 1981 to 1983 in an advertising agency. In 1984 he started his own business, which inspired his first picture book, *The Sleepy Owl,* published in 1986 by NordSüd. The big breakthrough followed in 1992 when Marcus Pfister wrote *The Rainbow Fish*–taking the bestseller lists by storm. To date, more than thirty million copies have been sold worldwide, in different formats, appearing in over fifty different languages. In his studio overlooking the Swiss capital, Marcus Pfister continues to create new characters and stories.

First published in Switzerland under the title *Der Regenbogenfisch lernt verlieren.*

Translated by David Henry Wilson.

First published in the United States, Great Britain, Canada, Australia, and New Zealand in 2012 by North-South Books Inc., an imprint of NordSüd Verlag AG, CH-8005 Zürich, Switzerland.
Distributed in the United States by North-South Books Inc., New York 10016.

Library of Congress Cataloging-in-Publication Data is available.
Printed in China
ISBN: 978-0-7358-4287-8
1 3 5 7 9 • 10 8 6 4 2
www.northsouth.com
www.rainbowfish.us
Meet Marcus Pfister at www.marcuspfister.ch

FSC
www.fsc.org
MIX
Paper from responsible sources
FSC® C007972

Marcus Pfister

You Can't Win Them All, RAINBOW FISH

Rainbow Fish enjoyed drifting around in the sea.

His home was the shining shoal, and he was happy there among his friends.

There had also been some additions to the shoal.

Red Fin had joined them, and immediately she and Rainbow Fish became good friends.

"Come on, let's play hide-and-seek," said Red Fin. "Will you be the first seeker, Rainbow Fish?"

Rainbow Fish agreed. He began to count up to twenty while the other fish looked for hiding places.
"I'm coming!" he shouted. "I'll find you in a fishy flash! I hope you're well hidden."
Rainbow Fish looked around. By now he knew most of the hiding places, so he knew exactly what to do and where to go.
But this time he couldn't find anybody.

There, among the algae, wasn't that something moving?
Rainbow Fish swam closer without taking his eyes off the area around him.
"I'm over here!" Red Fin shouted laughingly from behind. "You swam right past me!"
"Where were you? I never even saw you," said Rainbow Fish mystified.
"Not telling," said Red Fin. "Go and look for the others."

Rainbow Fish swam off toward the reef.
He searched and searched among the corals, and then at last . . .

“Hellooo! You didn’t see me! I’m over here!” cried the fish with the jagged fins.

Rainbow Fish had missed finding him too.

The only one missing now was Little Blue.

Hmmm. Rainbow Fish had already searched all around the reef, behind the corals, and in the algae. The only place left was among the sea anemones.

"Just you wait, Little Blue, I'll find you. . . ."

"Where are you going? I'm hiding over here!" cried Little Blue.

"I don't believe this," Rainbow Fish thought. "I didn't find a single one! This has never happened to me before!"

But he kept his frustration to himself and said, "Your turn to be seeker, Little Blue."

Rainbow Fish was pleased with himself now.

Little Blue would never find him. Little Blue was still very young and didn't have much experience playing hide-and-seek.

"One, two, three . . . ," Little Blue began to count while the other fish hid themselves.

Rainbow Fish ducked down behind a bush of algae and didn't move a muscle.

"Rainbow Fish, I can see you! You're hiding behind the algae!" cried Little Blue. "Come on out, Rainbow Fish. I've found you."

"I don't believe it!" said Rainbow Fish. "You can't possibly have seen me. You obviously didn't count up to twenty. It's not fair!"

All the other fish came out of their hiding places.

"Oh, come on, Rainbow Fish, it's only a game," said Red Fin, giving him a friendly poke in the ribs.

"What? Well, I think it's a dumb game, and I'm not playing!" said Rainbow Fish angrily, and he swam away.

“Can’t we play anymore?” asked Little Blue sadly. “I’m sorry, I was only trying to . . .”

“It’s not your fault, Little Blue,” said Red Fin. “You didn’t do anything wrong. I’ll talk to him. Don’t worry. Everything is going to be all right.”

Red Fin found Rainbow Fish near the reef.

"You were really unlucky this time, weren't you?" said Red Fin gently. "But you can't always win. It's only a game. And did you see the look in Little Blue's eyes? He was so proud that he'd found you. He's the one who always loses. And now you've spoiled all the fun for him. That's not fair."

Rainbow Fish listened in silence.

He knew Red Fin was right.

First, the other fish had simply found better hiding places than he had. Then he hadn't hidden himself well enough, and finally he'd been a poor sport.

"You're right." Rainbow Fish sighed. "I was acting like a poor sport. So now what do I do?"

"Come with me, apologize, and carry on with the game," said Red Fin warmly. "What else can you do?"

"I don't know if I'm brave enough to do that. It's all so embarrassing," said Rainbow Fish miserably.

"I know you pretty well," said Red Fin. "You know what you have to do. You'll make everything right again."

Together they went back to their friends. Rainbow Fish swam up to Little Blue.

"I'm sorry I was a poor sport, Little Blue. You're really good at hide-and-seek now. And I have to get used to it. . . . Will you give me another chance?"

"Yes!" said Little Blue with a big smile.

"My turn to count!" cried the fish with the jagged fins. "I'll find you in a fishy flash! I hope you're well hidden."

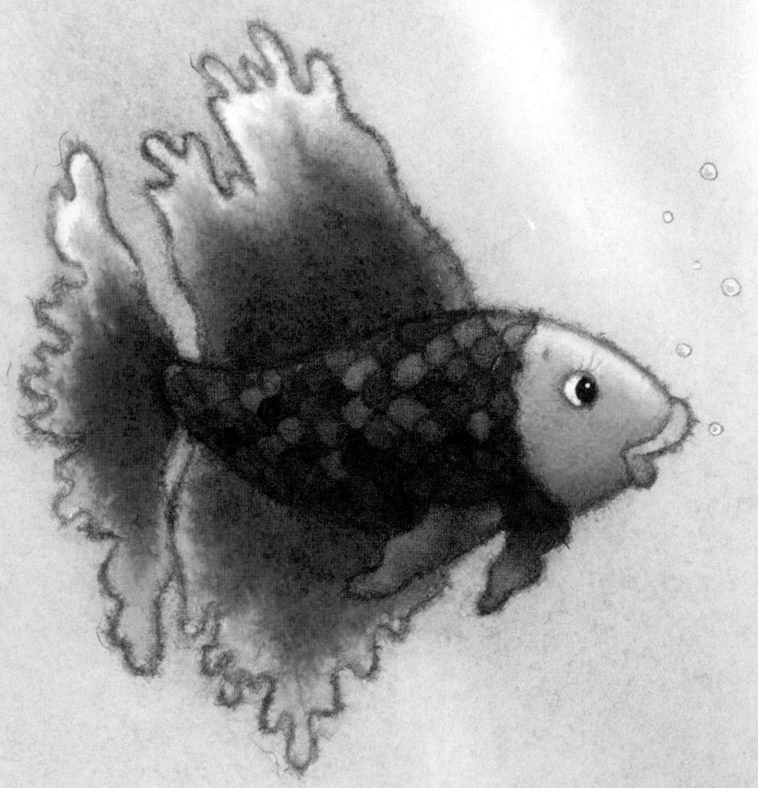